This Book belongs to

—Mrs. Bearss

Earthquakes

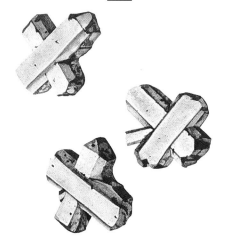

Text: Sharon Dalgleish
Consultant: Richard Whitaker, Senior Meteorologist,
Bureau of Meteorology, Sydney, Australia

This edition first published 2003 by
Mason Crest Publishers Inc.
370 Reed Road
Broomall, PA 19008

© Weldon Owen Inc.
Conceived and produced by
Weldon Owen Pty Limited

Library of Congress Cataloging-in-Publication Data
on file at the Library of Congress
ISBN: 1-59084-187-5

Printed in Singapore.
1 2 3 4 5 6 7 8 9 06 05 04 03

CONTENTS

Myths and Legends   4

Moving Continents   6

Driving Force   8

The Ocean Floor   10

Famous Earthquakes   12

Be Prepared   16

Warning Systems   18

Quake!   20

Tsunamis   26

Glossary   30

Index   31

MYTHS AND LEGENDS

For thousands of years, people from different cultures have told stories to explain volcanic eruptions and earthquakes. According to an ancient Hindu myth illustrated on the right, the Earth is carried on the back of an elephant, which stands on a turtle that is balanced on a cobra. Whenever one moves, the Earth trembles and shakes. Many other stories blame these events on the anger of the gods or demons that live in volcanoes. Hundreds of years ago, the Aztecs of Mexico and the people of Nicaragua even sacrificed young girls to the powerful gods they believed lived in lava lakes.

FLEA QUAKES
An old story from Siberia tells how the god Tuli carries the Earth on a sled pulled by flea-ridden dogs. Whenever the dogs stop to scratch, the Earth shakes!

STRANGE BUT TRUE

In 1660, little black crosses rained down on Naples. People thought it was proof that St. Januarius was looking after them. The crosses were really twinned crystals hurled out of Mt. Vesuvius during an eruption.

On the Move

Some plates move apart, some plates come together, and some collide. The arrows show the direction in which the main plates move.

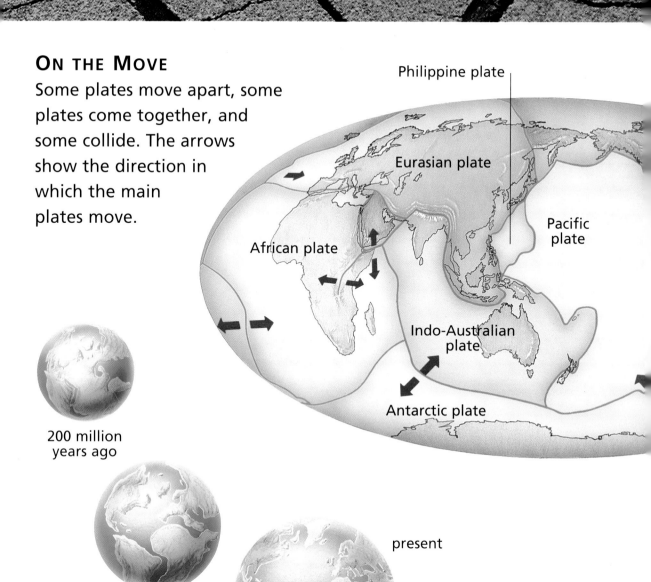

Philippine plate

Eurasian plate

Pacific plate

African plate

Indo-Australian plate

Antarctic plate

200 million years ago

90 million years ago

present

A Changing Planet

About 200 million years ago there was a single "super continent." Plate movements slowly split it into two land masses, and then into the continents we know today.

60 million years from now

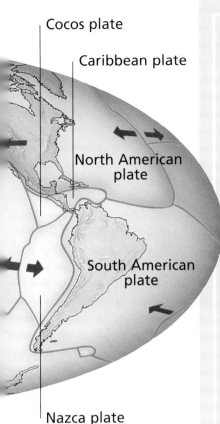

Cocos plate

Caribbean plate

North American plate

South American plate

Nazca plate

WHEN PLATES COLLIDE

1 Cut a paper plate in half. Imagine that these halves are two of the Earth's plates.

2 Using tape, attach a sheet of paper to the plate halves. Imagine that this paper is the Earth's crust.

3 Slide one plate half under the other. Did the paper buckle? That's what happens when two of the Earth's plates collide. The crust folds and mountains are formed.

MOVING CONTINENTS

The Earth's outermost section is made up of jagged slabs called plates. The plates fit together like a giant jigsaw puzzle. On top of each plate is a crust that lies under either an ocean, a continent, or a bit of both. You can't feel it, but these plates are always pulling and pushing against each other. It's along the edges where these plates meet that most earthquakes and volcanoes happen.

DRIVING FORCE

The Earth is shaped like a big ball. Inside are layers made of different materials. The crust and plates on the outside float on a squishy layer of soft rock. The center of the Earth is called the core. The core is very hot—temperatures can reach more than 8,000 degrees Fahrenheit (4,400 degrees Celsius)! This heat causes strong currents, as hot rock moves up and cold rock sinks. These currents make the giant plates move across the surface of the Earth. As they move, they cause earthquakes and volcanic eruptions, and form mountains and islands.

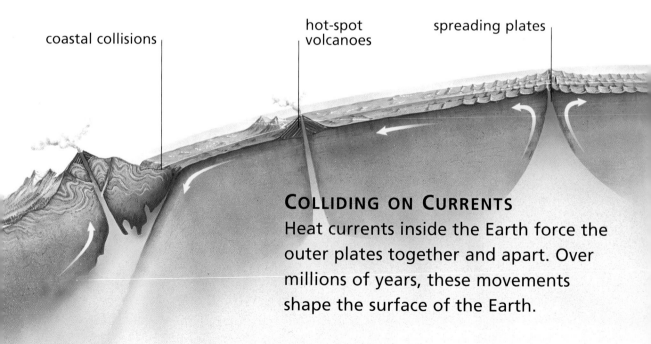

coastal collisions

hot-spot volcanoes

spreading plates

COLLIDING ON CURRENTS
Heat currents inside the Earth force the outer plates together and apart. Over millions of years, these movements shape the surface of the Earth.

AMAZING!

More than 500,000 earthquakes happen every year. Thankfully, most of these are too weak to cause the sort of damage shown here.

SHAKING BUILDINGS

When the edges of sliding plates grind past each other, stress builds up in the rocks and the ground can start to shake. The buildings on top will shake, too!

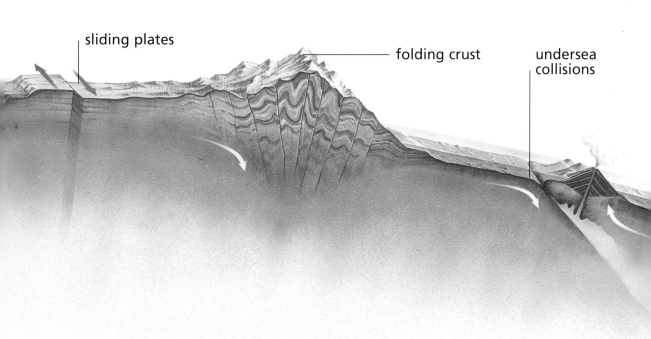

sliding plates

folding crust

undersea collisions

BLACK SMOKERS

Volcanic chimneys up to 11 yards (10 meters) high are found along spreading ridges on the ocean floor.

Smoking Chimneys
Minerals build up on the sides of vents to make natural chimneys.

Moving Water
Cold water seeps down through the ridge. Magma heats it before it rises back up the vent.

Sea Floor Cracks
As two plates with ocean crust move apart, a crack or rift forms.

Filling the Cracks
Magma rises to fill the crack between the two plates.

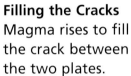

New Edges
Magma cools and hardens, and adds to the edges of the plates.

THE OCEAN FLOOR

When two plates with ocean crust move apart, magma bubbles up to fill the rift. The magma cools and hardens to make new strips of ocean floor at the edges of the plates. The Atlantic Ocean is widening like this by 0.8 inches (2 centimeters) every year. When one of these spreading ridges breaks, an earthquake happens. Volcanoes can also form in the ridges. Over millions of years the volcanoes can grow so big that they rise above the water as islands.

DID YOU KNOW?

In 1906, a massive earthquake shook San Francisco. Buildings crumbled and fires burned for three days. About 1,000 people died and 300,000 were left homeless.

FAMOUS EARTHQUAKES

A major earthquake could strike California at any time. This North American state straddles two plates. The grating movement of the plates has caused a weblike series of faults and cracks in the crust. The most famous is the San Andreas Fault. From time to time, the rock breaks and moves along part of the fault. This can trigger an earthquake. Scientists record more than 20,000 earth tremors in California every year.

TRAPPED
Earthquakes can collapse freeways, trapping people in the wreckage.

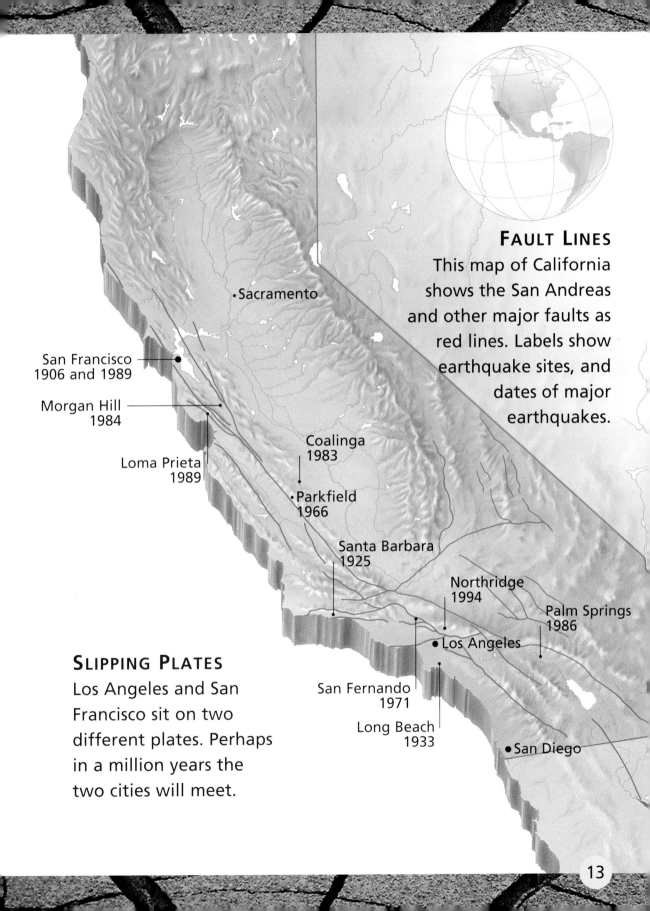

FAULT LINES
This map of California shows the San Andreas and other major faults as red lines. Labels show earthquake sites, and dates of major earthquakes.

•Sacramento

San Francisco
1906 and 1989

Morgan Hill
1984

Loma Prieta
1989

Coalinga
1983

•Parkfield
1966

Santa Barbara
1925

Northridge
1994

Palm Springs
1986

•Los Angeles

SLIPPING PLATES
Los Angeles and San Francisco sit on two different plates. Perhaps in a million years the two cities will meet.

San Fernando
1971

Long Beach
1933

•San Diego

When a massive earthquake struck Mexico City in 1985, more than 10,000 people were killed and 50,000 injured. As the Cocos plate slipped under the North American plate, it cracked more than 12 miles (20 kilometers) down inside the Earth. The vibrations caused shock waves with 1,000 times more energy than an atomic bomb. These shock waves traveled nearly 218 miles (350 kilometers) east to Mexico City. Many buildings in the city collapsed or were badly damaged. Rescue workers searched nonstop for days after the earthquake. They rescued more than 4,000 people in the wreckage.

ON SHAKY GROUND

Mexico City lies near an area where a number of plates meet. This area is a section of what scientists call the Pacific Ring of Fire.

North American plate

Caribbean plate

Mexico City

Cocos plate

Pacific plate

Nazca plate

South American plate

STRANGE BUT TRUE

A four-day old baby boy survived for nine days buried under the rubble of a hospital. Here, the baby is lifted to safety by rescue workers.

15

BE PREPARED

When an earthquake strikes, beware of falling buildings and flying objects! Earthquake drills are part of daily life for school children in quake-prone areas. Cities in these areas also have strict rules to follow when repairing old buildings or designing new ones. Walls, floors, roofs, and foundations are reinforced. Heavy furniture is bolted to walls to keep it from flying around. Some areas even have gas lines that bend instead of breaking under pressure.

Drop!
Each child crouches under a desk with one arm around its leg to hold it down.

SINKING BUILDINGS
In an earthquake, buildings on loose soil sink or fall over because they have no support.

STRANGE BUT TRUE

This rocket-shaped building in San Francisco is designed to be "earthquake proof." The base is built on a concrete raft that gives extra support when shock waves pass through.

Safety Measures
In some places, computers are bolted to tables, and bookshelves are attached to walls.

WARNING SYSTEMS

Every 30 seconds the Earth shakes slightly. Most of these tremors are too small to be felt by humans. Scientists monitor active earthquake areas around the world. They use different equipment—from bottles of water to NASA satellites—to detect and measure any movements or changes in the ground. With enough warning, people can be evacuated before an earthquake hits. Even with these warning systems, earthquakes are still unpredictable and often much stronger than expected.

DID YOU KNOW?

Many people believe that animals have a secret sense for detecting earthquakes. Scientists have studied catfish in Japan and beetles in California, but there is still no proof.

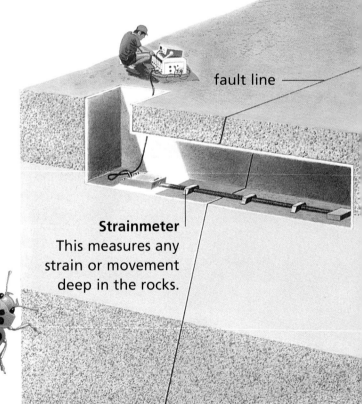

fault line

Strainmeter
This measures any strain or movement deep in the rocks.

Laser Beams
These bounce between Earth and a satellite and measure any large movements of the Earth's surface.

Satellite Dish
This picks up signals from outer space.

Seismometer
This detects, measures, and records any tremor in the ground.

Borehole Tiltmeter
This measures any change in the tilt of the ground deep under the surface.

Long Tiltmeter
This measures any change in the tilt of the ground at the surface.

Fires
Fires are often more dangerous than the earthquake.

QUAKE!

Earthquakes strike swiftly and suddenly, but the aftereffects can be even more dangerous. When the ground stops shaking, cut power lines can start fires, and fumes from broken gas lines can cause explosions. Lack of electricity means that lifesaving equipment cannot be used. Emergency centers for the injured and homeless are set up in undamaged areas, while rescue teams search for survivors buried under huge amounts of rubble.

EARTHQUAKE WAVES

The energy from an earthquake travels in waves through the rock. This wavy line is a typical printout from a seismometer during an earthquake.

Survivors
Searching for survivors is the first priority after an earthquake.

Normal Fault
The ground cracks as rocks are pulled apart. One side slides down the fault to a lower level.

Reverse Fault
The ground cracks as rocks are pushed together. One side slides up and over the other one to a higher level.

Strike-slip Fault
Rocks break and a block of land moves sideways.

The shift of rocks along a fault line causes violent shaking. This movement can be from side to side or up and down. This scene shows the damage to a road after an earthquake with these types of movement. Scientists measure earthquakes according to two scales. The Modified Mercalli scale measures the amount of shaking and damage during an earthquake. The Richter scale measures the amount, or magnitude, of energy released by an earthquake. The earthquake is then given a grade from 1 to 9 on the Richter scale.

RICHTER SCALE

Magnitude 1–2
Detected only by instruments. More than 500,000 a year.

Magnitude 2–3
Slightly felt by humans. 100,000 to 500,000 a year.

Magnitude 3–4
Lights might swing. Little damage. 10,000 to 100,000 a year.

Magnitude 4–5
Strongly felt. Some damage. 1,000 to 10,000 a year.

Magnitude 5–6
Felt very strongly. Walls crack. 200 to 1,000 a year.

Magnitude 6–7
Severely felt. Some buildings collapse. 20 to 200 a year.

Magnitude 7–8
Severely felt. Ground cracks. 10 to 20 a year.

Magnitude 8–9
Massive destruction. Up to 10 a year.

DANGER WITHIN

Sometimes the outside of a building survives an earthquake but the inside is badly damaged. Heavy furniture, appliances, and small flying objects can also cause serious injuries.

DID YOU KNOW?

In some earthquake-prone areas, dogs are trained to search for survivors in collapsed buildings.

During an earthquake disaster, emergency measures are needed to protect people's lives and property. Volunteers are often called in to help rescue teams. Some cities even have special disaster teams ready to jump into action. Many people living in these areas have prepared emergency supply kits with food, water, and medicine.

AIRLIFT TO SAFETY
In an earthquake-damaged city, helicopters are often the only reliable transportation for emergency services.

TSUNAMIS

Tsunamis (pronounced soo-nah-mees) are huge killer waves. Tsunamis are caused by a jolt to the ocean floor from an earthquake, volcanic eruption, or landslide. They are wide, moving mountains of water that reach all the way down to the seafloor and travel at great speeds for huge distances. A sharp rise in the ocean floor near a coastline acts as a brake at the bottom of the wave. The bottom of the wave is forced up in a towering wall of water.

WALL OF WATER
Thousands of years ago, part of one of the volcanic Hawaiian Islands collapsed into the sea. A 33-yard (30-meter) high tsunami crashed across the next island. If it happened today, 33-yard (30-meter) waves could roll into the city of Honolulu.

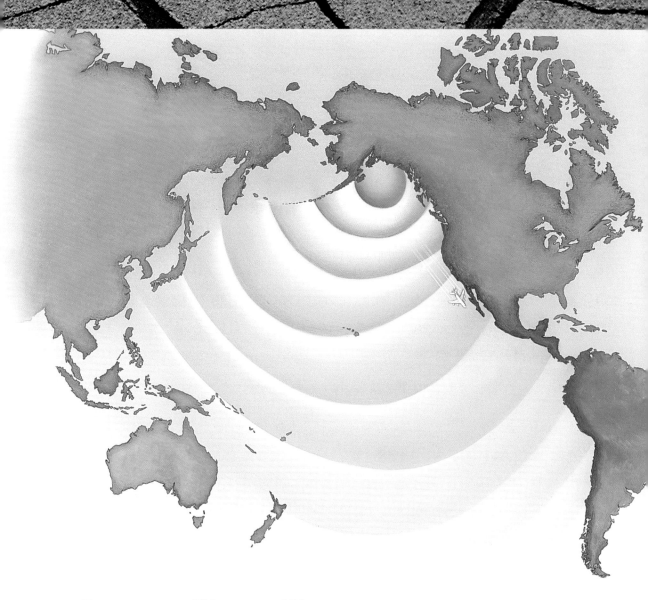

BUILDING A WALL OF WATER

The speed of a tsunami depends on how deep the ocean is. The wave gets higher and higher as it moves toward the more shallow water near land.

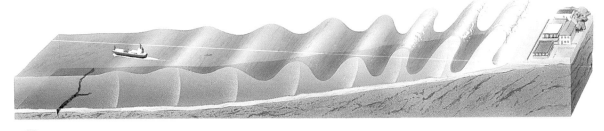

A tsunami can race across oceans at speeds of up to 500 miles (800 kilometers) per hour—as fast as a jet plane. That's why an earthquake in Alaska can trigger a tsunami with arcs that rapidly spread across the whole Pacific region. Most tsunamis occur in the Pacific area, so special detectors have been set up throughout the area to measure their travel time. People in danger can then be warned in time to escape. When a tsunami hits land, any people and buildings nearby are swept out to sea, and yet far out at sea, a tsunami may pass unnoticed under a ship.

PULLING THE PLUG

An approaching tsunami can cause the water to drain from a harbor. Don't stay to watch! The water will build up speed and height before rushing back to shore.

GLOSSARY

continent One of the seven main land masses of the globe.

crust The outer layer of the Earth.

fault A crack or break in the Earth's crust where rocks have shifted.

magma Molten rock inside the Earth.

Mercalli scale A scale that measures the amount of shaking during an earthquake.

Pacific Ring of Fire The area along the edges of the Pacific Ocean where many of the world's earthquakes and volcanoes occur.

plate One of the slabs of the Earth's outermost part.

Richter scale A scale that measures the amount of energy released by an earthquake. It is expressed in numerals between 1 and 9.

ridge A long mountain.

tsunami A wave that is produced by a movement in the ocean floor caused by an earthquake, volcanic eruption, or undersea landslide.

vents Openings in the Earth's crust that allow built-up gases and heat to escape into the water or air.

INDEX

aftereffects	20, 24
detecting earthquakes	18–19
earthquake drills	16
Earth's core	8
Earth's crust	7, 8, 9, 11, 12
fault lines	12, 13, 18, 22
measuring earthquakes	18, 22–23
Modified Mercalli Scale	22
Pacific Ring of Fire	15
plates	6–7, 8–9, 11, 13, 14, 15
Richter scale	22, 23
San Andreas Fault	12, 13
search dogs	24
super continent	6
tsunamis	26–29
underwater volcanoes	10–11
volcanic activity	4, 5, 7, 8, 10, 11, 27
volcanic chimneys	10

PICTURE AND ILLUSTRATION CREDITS

BOOKS IN THIS SERIES

WEIRD AND WONDERFUL WILDLIFE

Incredible Creatures
Creepy Creatures
Scaly Things
Feathers and Flight
Attack and Defense
Snakes
Hidden World
Reptiles and Amphibians
Mini Mammals
Up and Away
Mighty Mammals
Dangerous Animals

LAND, SEA, AND SKY

Sharks and Rays
Underwater Animals
Mammals of the Sea
Ocean Life
Volcanoes
Weather Watching
Maps and Our World
Earthquakes
The Plant Kingdom
Rain or Shine
Sky Watch
The Planets

INFORMATION STATION

Every Body Tells a Story
The Human Body
Bright Ideas
Out and About
Exploring Space
High Flying
How Things Work
Native Americans
Travelers and Traders
Sports for All
People from the Past
Play Ball!